To Ada
Mrs Robertson

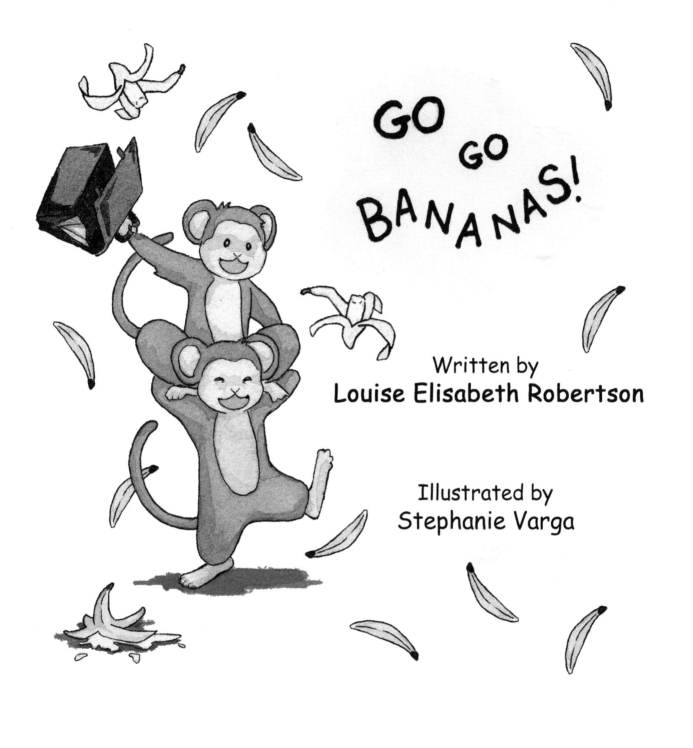

GO GO BANANAS!

Written by
Louise Elisabeth Robertson

Illustrated by
Stephanie Varga

For our collective bunch of bananas

TIFFANY, BRITTANY, FREDDIE,DOUGLAS, CHARLIE, FIONA,

I love you all!!

SOME THINGS DRIVE ME

CRAZY HAPPY,

AND SOME THINGS DRIVE ME CRAZY MAD,

AND SOMETIMES EVEN

JUST A LITTLE SAD.

WHEN DAD SAYS, "WHO WANTS TO GO ON A FAB, FUN HOLIDAY?"

"HEY, LET'S GET READY TO GO ON SATURDAY!"

WHEN I KEEP HAVING TO BEND DOWN TO TIE MY SHOE,

OR WHEN THERE IS NO PAPER IN THE LOO!

5

THAT MAKES ME WANT TOOO...
GO GO BANANAS!
WHAT ABOUT YOU?
LET'S GO GO BANANAS!
I'LL GO BANANAS,
YOU GO BANANAS,
SOAP
WE'LL ALL GO BANANAS TOO!

WHEN MUM SAYS, "HEY, LET'S GO TO THE TOWN FUN FAIR!"

"MAYBE WE'LL GET SOME

CRAZY FUN SCARE!"

8

WHEN I NEED A DOLLAR OR A DIME,

A PENNY OR A POUND,

THEN I'M SO LUCKY AND SPOT ONE
ON THE GROUND!

9

THAT MAKES ME WANT TOOO...
GO GO BANANAS!
WHAT ABOUT YOU?
LET'S GO GO BANANAS!
I'LL GO BANANAS,
YOU GO BANANAS,
WE'LL ALL GO BANANAS TOO!

WHEN THERE'S TOO MUCH UNNECESSARY RUBBISH OR WASTE,

OR MY SISTER LEAVES THE LID OFF THE TOOTHPASTE!

11

WHEN I'M STANDING AT THE RAILWAY STATION

AND THE TRAIN IS EXTREMELY LATE!

THEN I ACCIDENTALLY DROP MY KEY DOWN THE GRATE!

13

WHEN I GET A REALLY COOL

FACE PAINT,

AND THE RAIN BECOMES

RATHER FAINT!

15

WHEN DAD EXCLAIMS,

"NO MORE EATING THAT CANDY!"

AND THEN I SNEEZE AND THERE'S NO TISSUE HANDY!

WHEN I GET INVITED TO AN

AMAZING BIRTHDAY PARTY,

AND I GET THE CHANCE TO BE INCREDIBLY ARTY!

19

WHEN I GET GUM
STUCK ON MY SHOE,

OR I HAVE FAR TOO MUCH
HOMEWORK TO DO!

WHEN I GET TO BAKE
A DELICIOUS CAKE,

I HOPE EATING IT ALL WON'T
GIVE ME A BELLYACHE!

WHEN THE WEATHER OUTSIDE IS

INCREDIBLY GLOOMY,

AND MY SISTER SEEMS

RATHER MOODY!

WHEN I SNUGGLE INTO

MY SLEEPY BED,

AND SOMEONE WHO LOVES ME

TUCKS ME UP AND KISSES MY HEAD!

27

29

Louise E Robertson (FRSA, MSc, B'Ed, PGC) Born in Northamptonshire UK. Louise is a successful educator, and has been a Head Teacher in three schools. As leader of leadership teams in schools in England, Scotland and Indonesia, she has always loved books for children. Louise currently lives between the UK and the USA, and is now writing for children. She is married to Frank and between them they have six children.

Stephanie Varga is a recent graduate of North Central College with a double major in Studio Art and Japanese. Raised in Bloomingdale, IL, she has always been fascinated with telling stories with pictures in many forms.